For Ceilidh, my wee bundle
of plans and patience

LADYBIRD BOOKS

UK | USA | Canada | Ireland | Australia
India | New Zealand | South Africa

Ladybird Books is part of the Penguin Random House group of companies
whose addresses can be found at global.penguinrandomhouse.com.

www.penguin.co.uk   www.puffin.co.uk   www.ladybird.co.uk

 Penguin
Random House
UK

First published 2019 by Nancy Paulsen Books,
an imprint of Penguin Random House LLC, New York, USA
This edition published in Great Britain by Ladybird Books Ltd 2022
001

Original design by Marikka Tamura
Text hand-lettered by Cinders McLeod

Printed in China

The authorized representative in the EEA is Penguin Random House Ireland,
Morrison Chambers, 32 Nassau Street, Dublin D02 YH68

A CIP catalogue record for this book is available from the British Library

ISBN: 978-0-241-52751-1

All correspondence to:
Ladybird Books, Penguin Random House Children's
One Embassy Gardens, 8 Viaduct Gardens
London SW11 7BW

This is
Honey.

This is →
Honey's
dad.

These are Honey's
5 siblings. ↓

This is the money
Honey DREAMS
of saving.

(inside the bag)

Carrots are money
in Bunnyland.

Honey earns 2 carrots a week
for taking care of
her siblings.

It's a lot of work to watch them all!

They are

LOUD

and BOUNCY.

Gaa!

Buh
buh
buh!

Oh boy, I want my

So I can get some

# PEACE

and

# QUIET!

Whee!

Wheee!

Well, maybe you could save for one?

Won't that take
FOREVER?

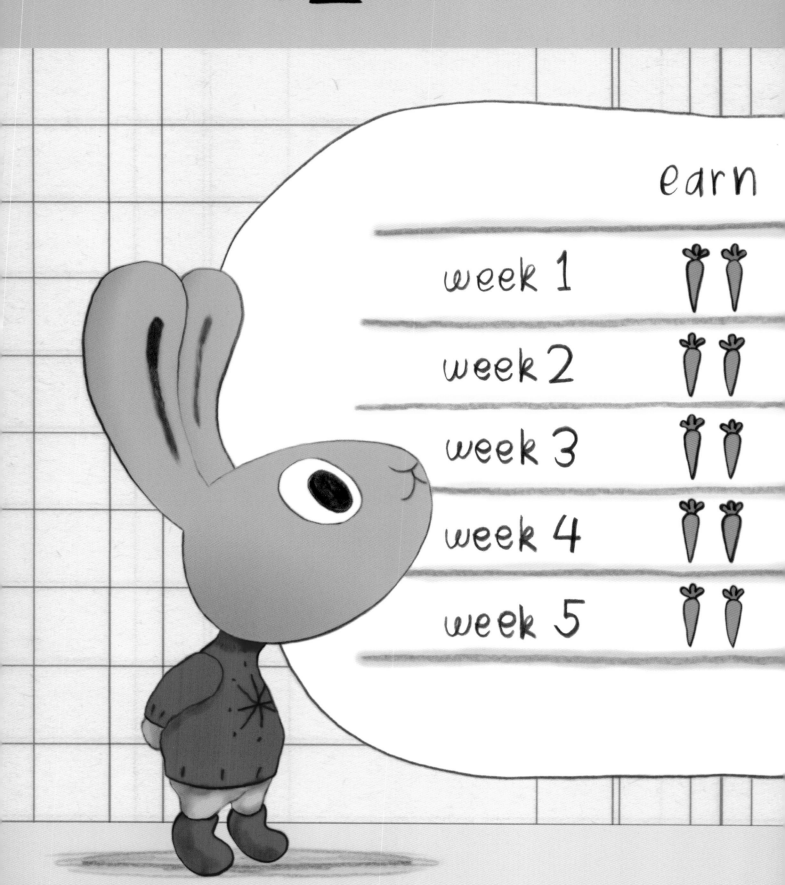

Hmm. Saving **2** carrots a week means

earn

week 1

week 2

week 3

week 4

week 5

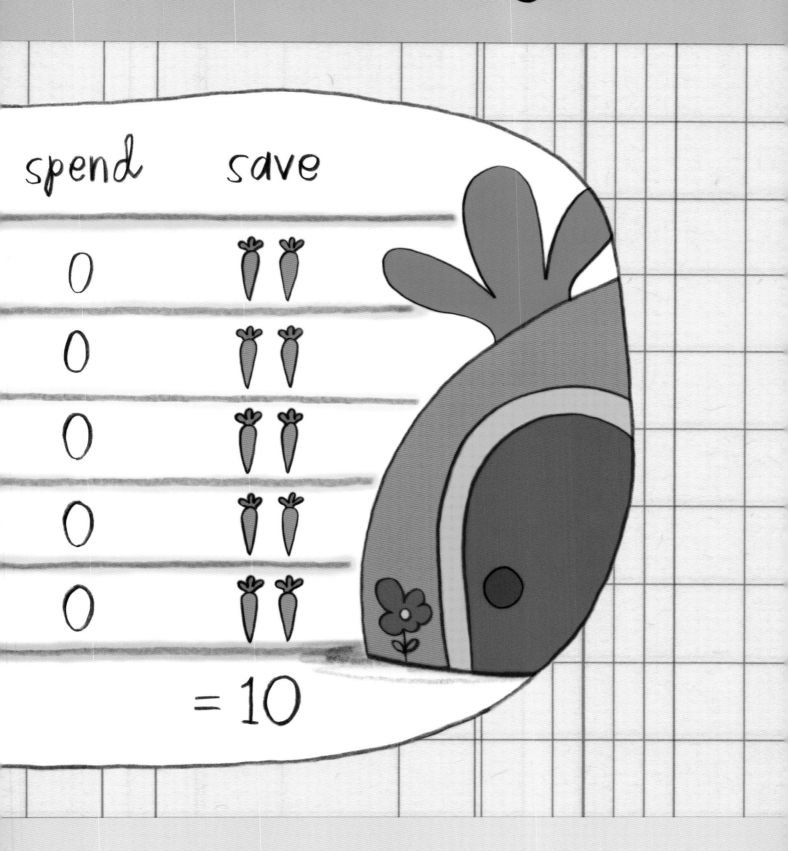

spend    save

0    🥕 🥕

0    🥕 🥕

0    🥕 🥕

0    🥕 🥕

0    🥕 🥕

= 10

But, if all I do is
SAVE,
I can't buy ice cream
or go to the movies!
That's no fun!

Well,
it's your money, Honey.
What do you want
to do with it?

|  |  | earn | spend |
|---|---|---|---|
|  | week 1 | 🥕 🥕 | 🥕 |
|  | week 2 | 🥕 🥕 | 🥕 |
|  | week 3 | 🥕 🥕 | 🥕 |
|  | week 4 | 🥕 🥕 | 🥕 |
|  | week 5 | 🥕 🥕 | 🥕 |
|  | week 6 | 🥕 🥕 | 🥕 |
|  | week 7 | 🥕 🥕 | 🥕 |
|  | week 8 | 🥕 🥕 | 🥕 |
|  | week 9 | 🥕 🥕 | 🥕 |
|  | week 10 | 🥕 🥕 | 🥕 |

# I'll do it !
And now when I watch my siblings,

I can dream of my playhouse!

10 weeks later...

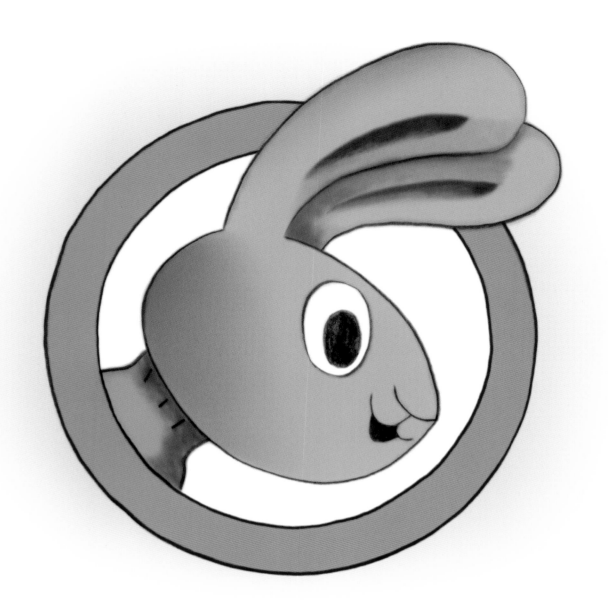

# HONEY, YOU DID IT!

you bought your playhouse
all by yourself!

Indoor voice, Dad!
This is my quiet place.

I saved and made my dream

# COME TRUE!

the end

# It's never too early to teach your little bunny about money!

## Collect all the books in the Moneybunny series:

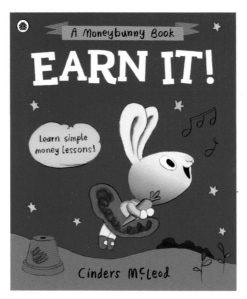

ISBN: 978−0−241−52749−8

ISBN: 978−0−241−52752−8

✓ ISBN: 978−0−241−52751−1

ISBN: 978−0−241−52750−4